ABCDEFG
HIJKLMN
OPQRST
UVWXYZ

W0082447

A is for AORTA

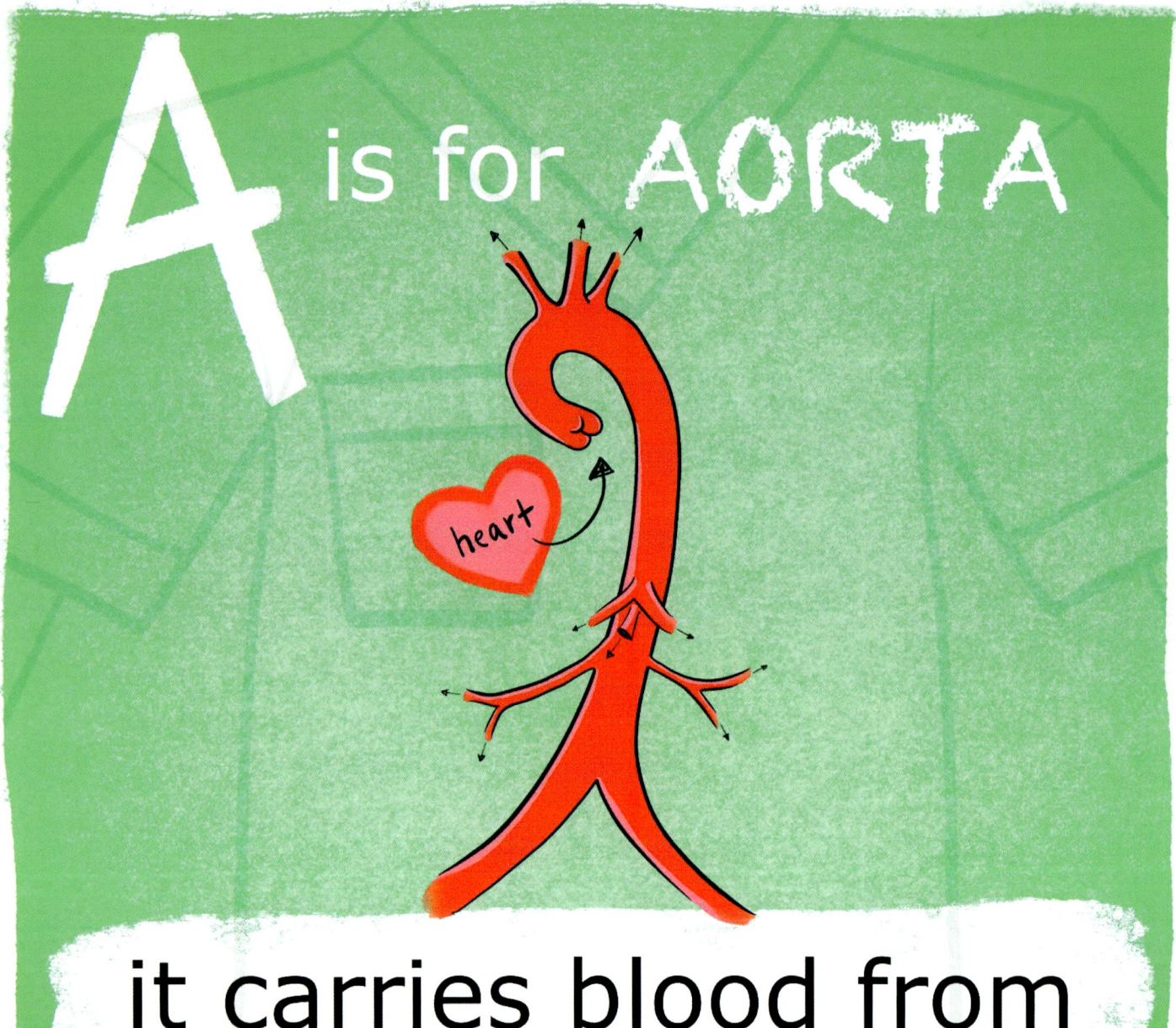

it carries blood from your heart

B is for BONE MARROW

red

yellow

which is where blood cells get their start

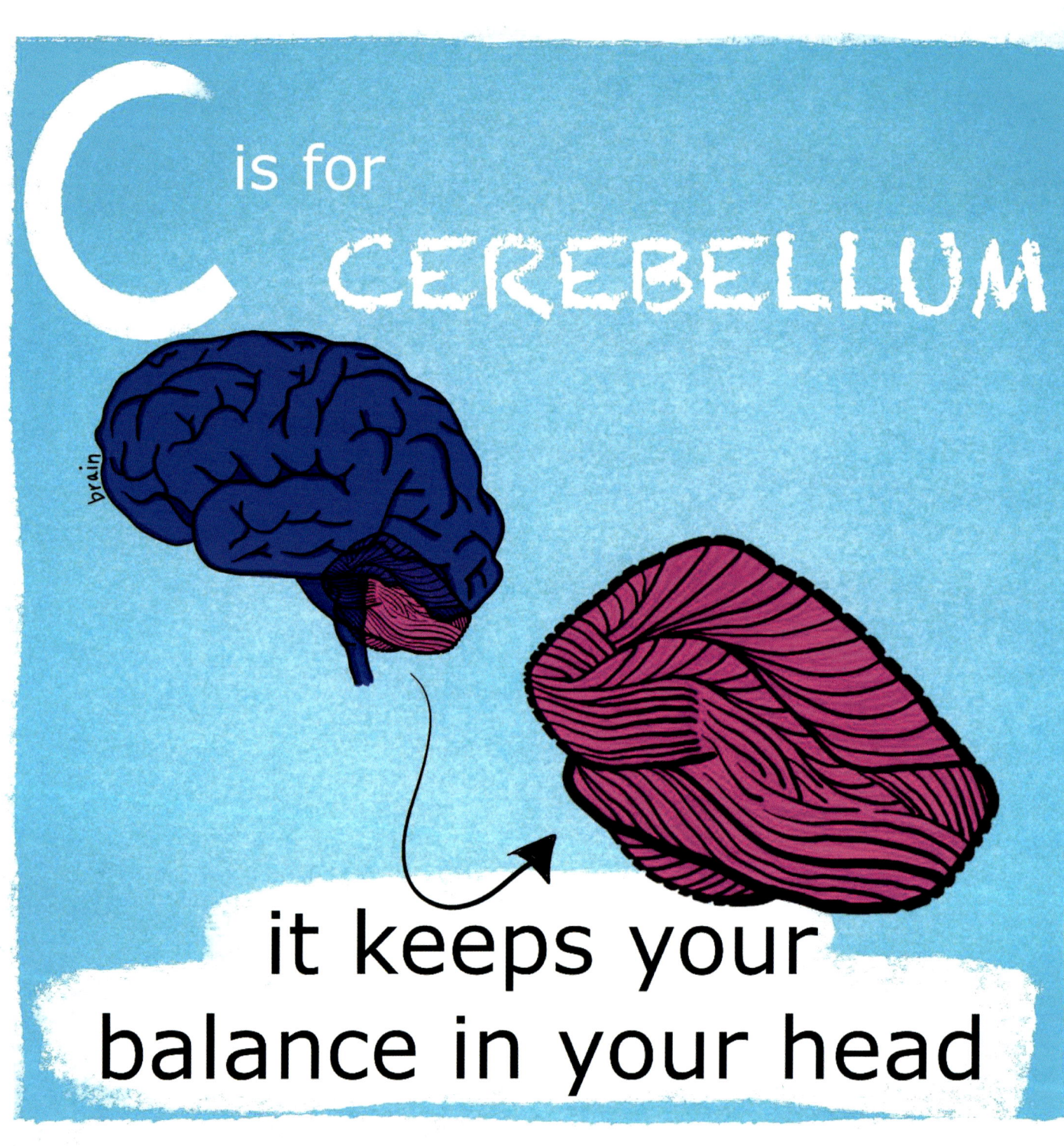

D is for DUODENUM

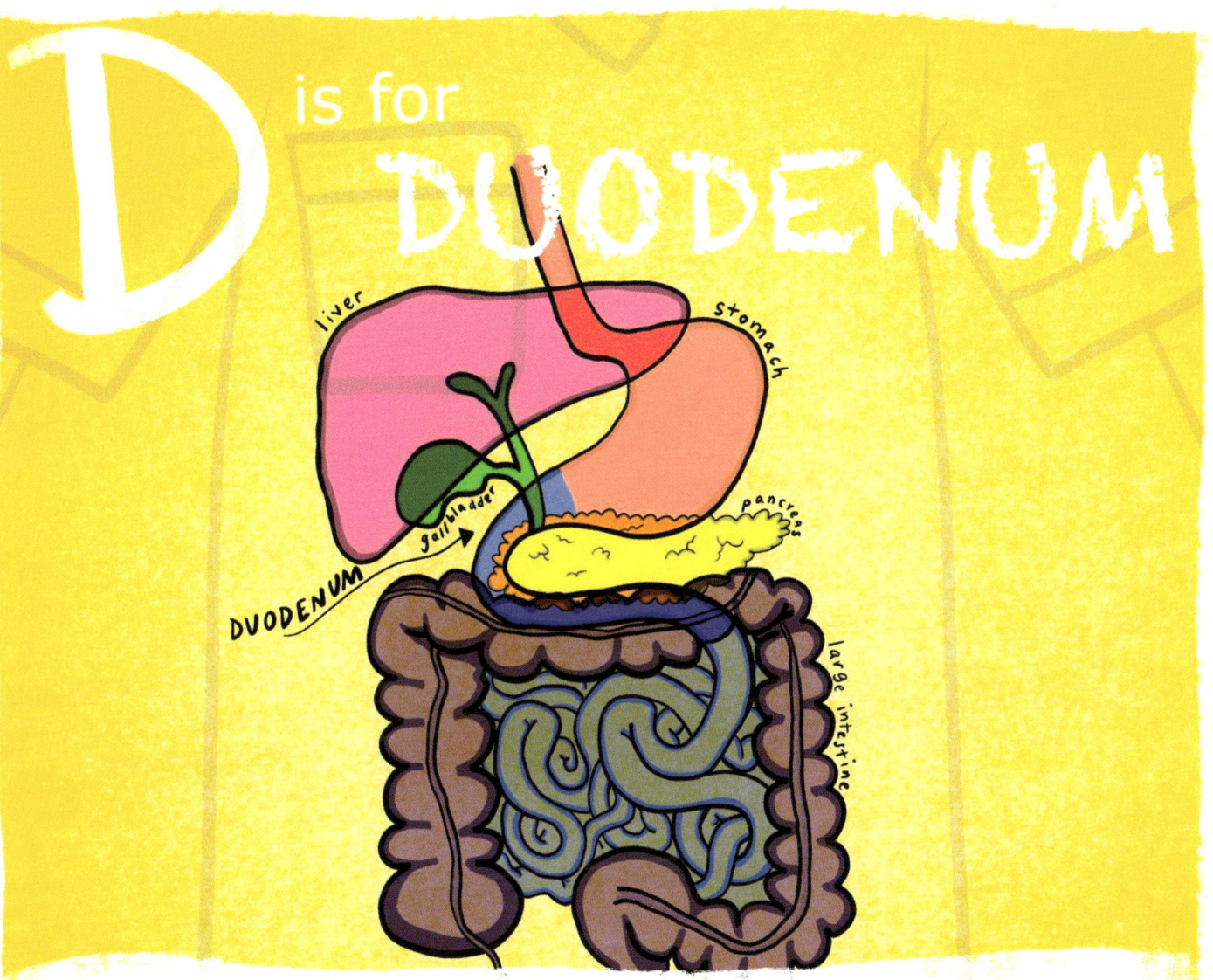

which helps break down
what you were fed

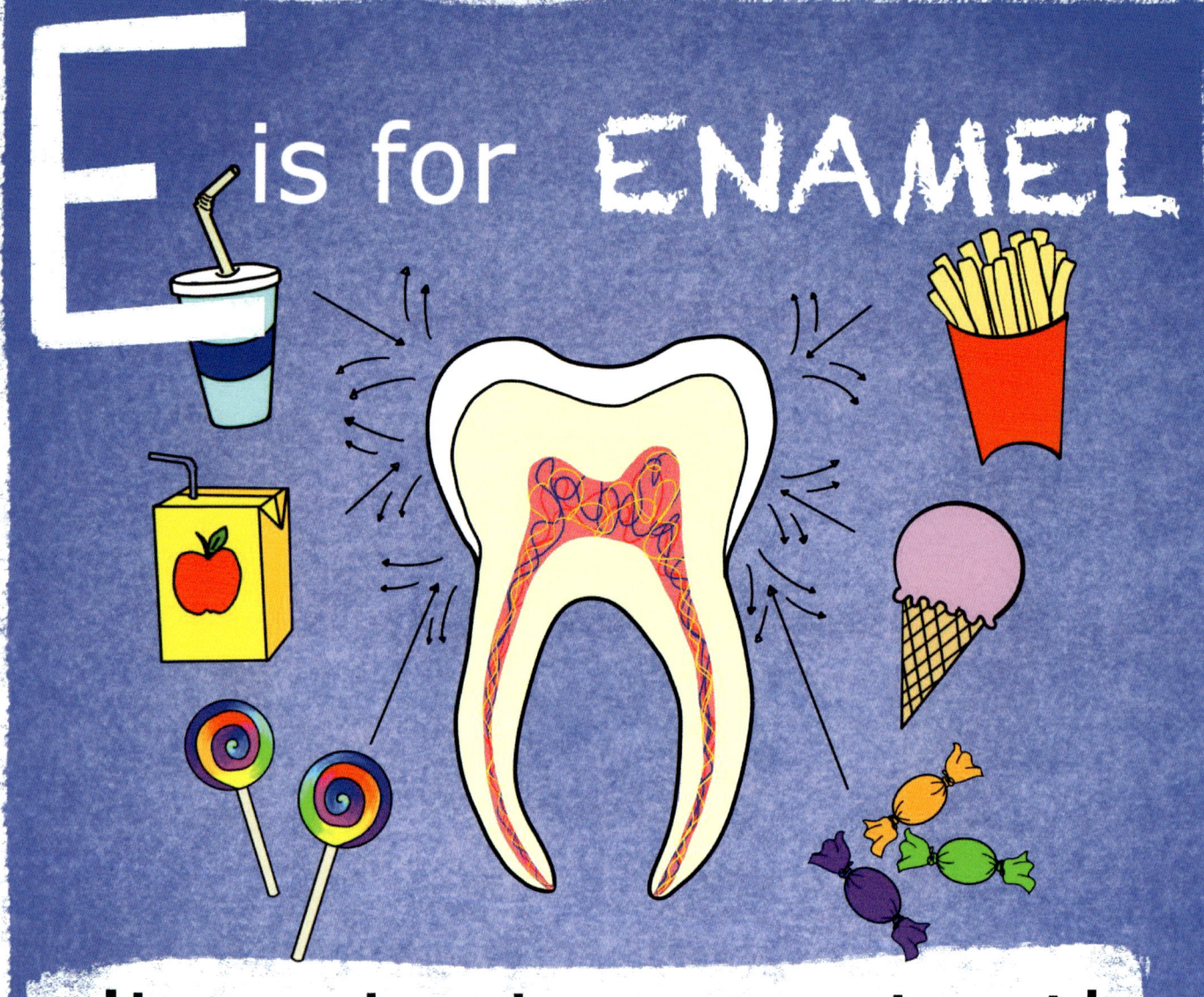

E is for ENAMEL

it protects your teeth from junk

F
is for FRONTAL LOBE

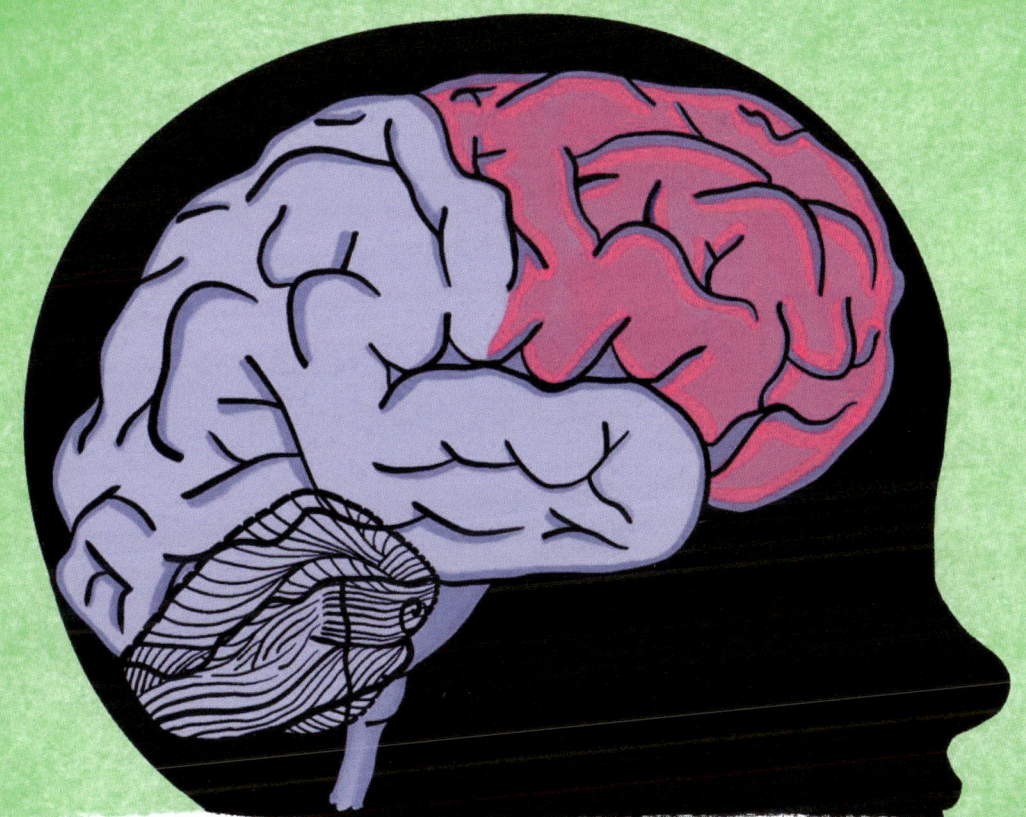

which filters thoughts
you have thunk

G is for GALLBLADDER

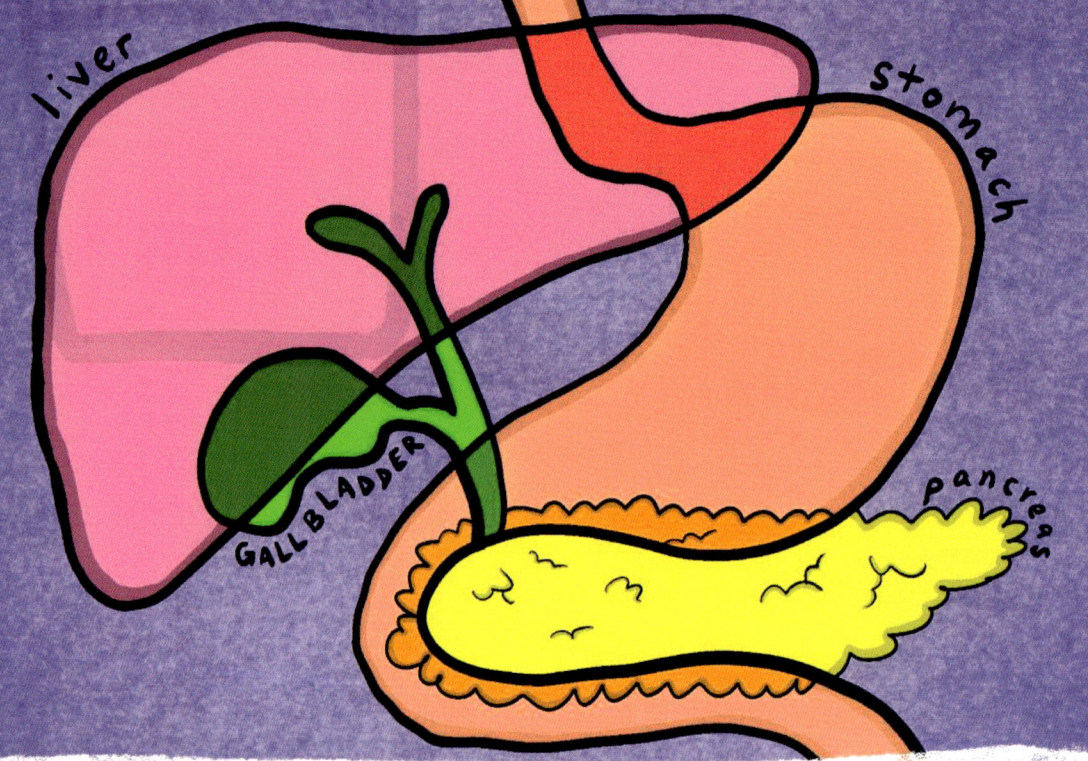

it stores your yucky green bile

H is for HYOID

which is a bone that helps you smile

I is for IRIS

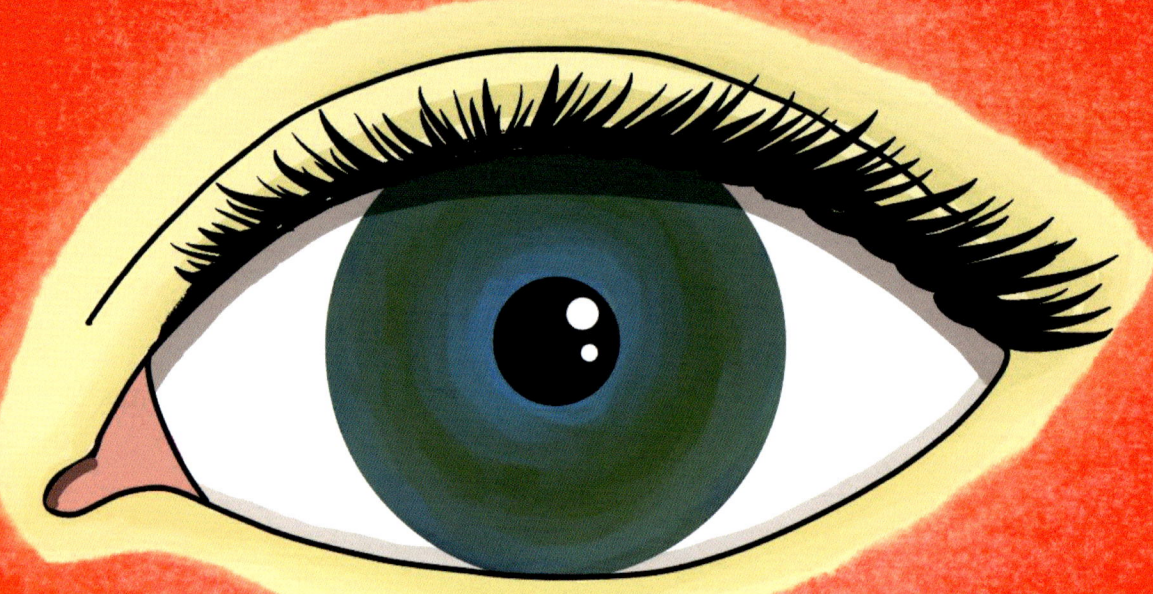

it gives color to your eyes

J is for JOINTS

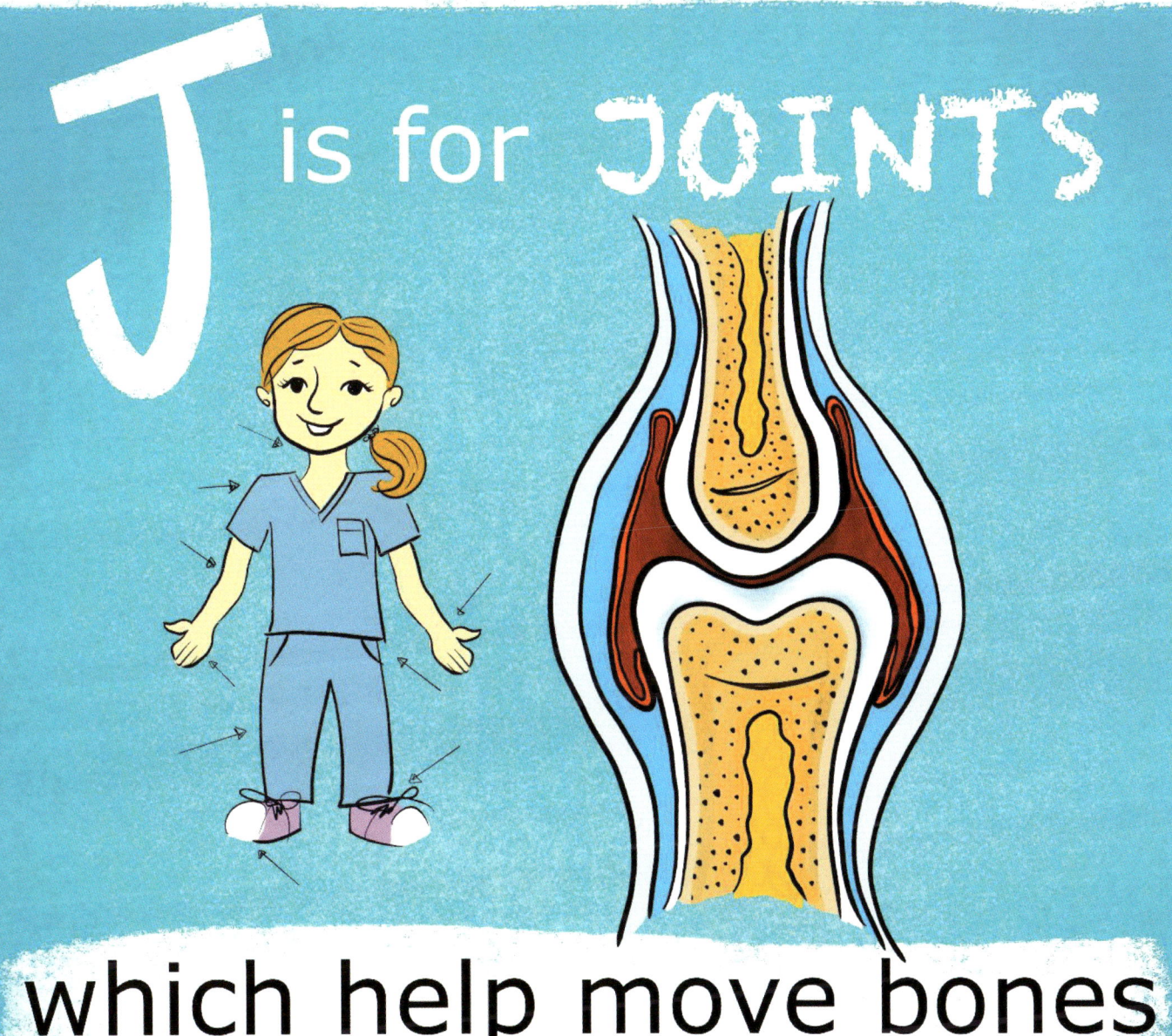

which help move bones of any size

K is for KIDNEY

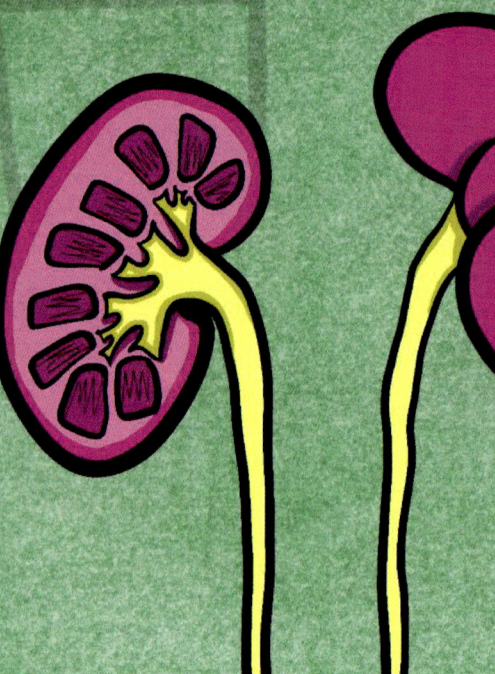

it filters blood and makes your pee

L is for LUNGS

which take oxygen in
for you and me

M is for MASSETER

it helps you chew your veggies and fruits

N is for NARES

which flare when someone toots

O is for OPTIC NERVE

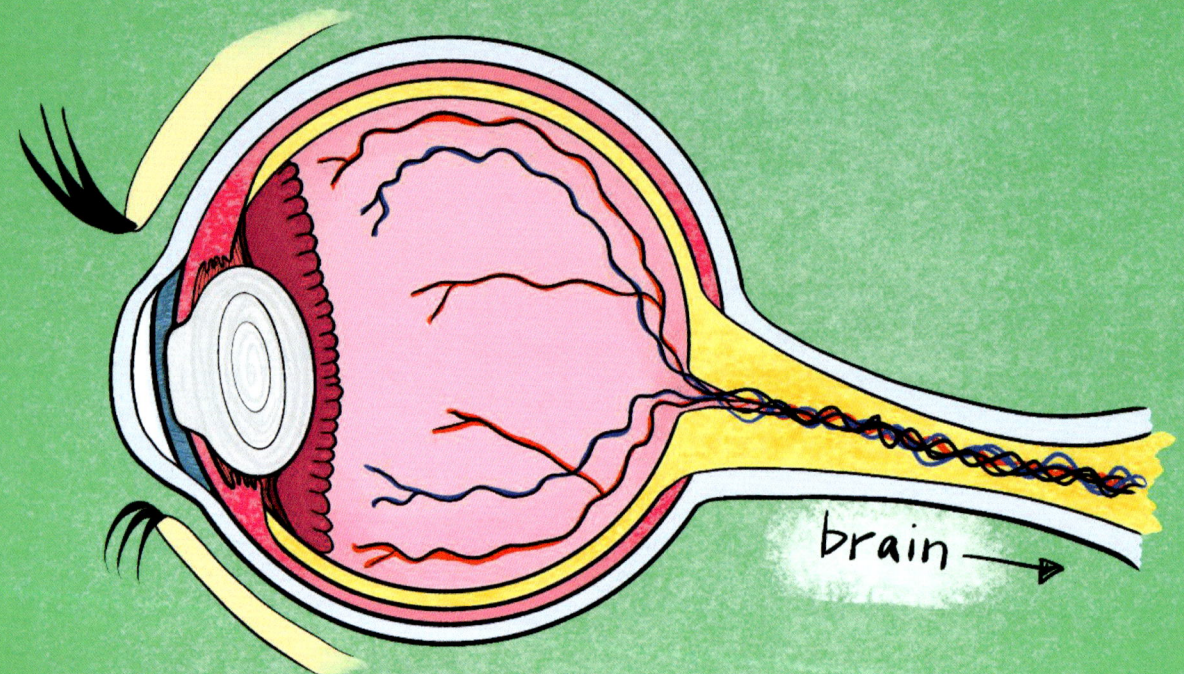

brain →

it tells your brain
what you see

P is for PATELLA

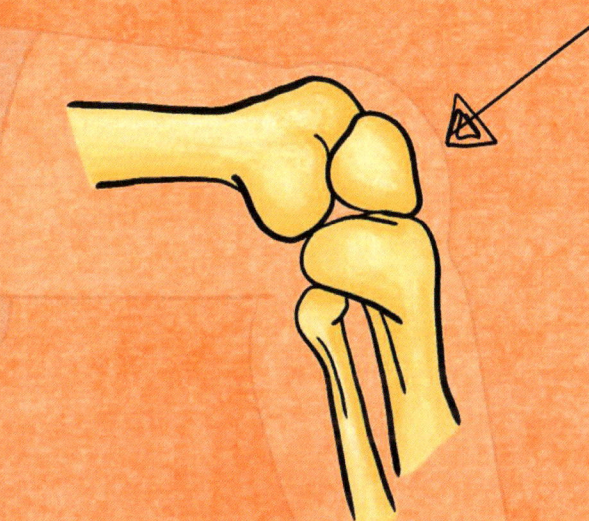

which is the cap on your knee

Q is for QUADRICEP

it's the strongest muscle in your thigh

R is for RIBS

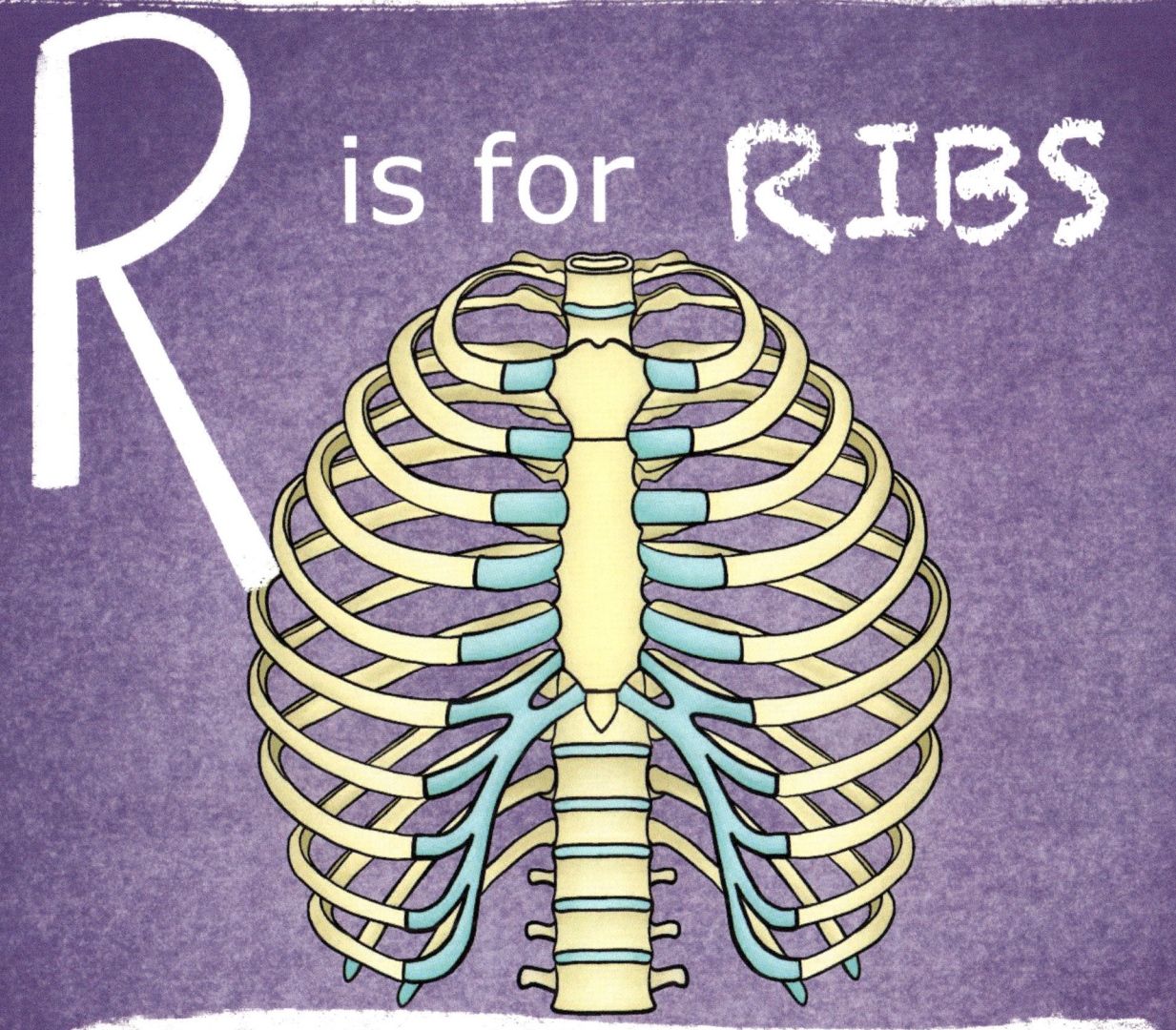

which expand when you take a deep sigh

S is for SPLEEN

its job is to get rid
of old blood cells

T is for TYMPANIC MEMBRANE

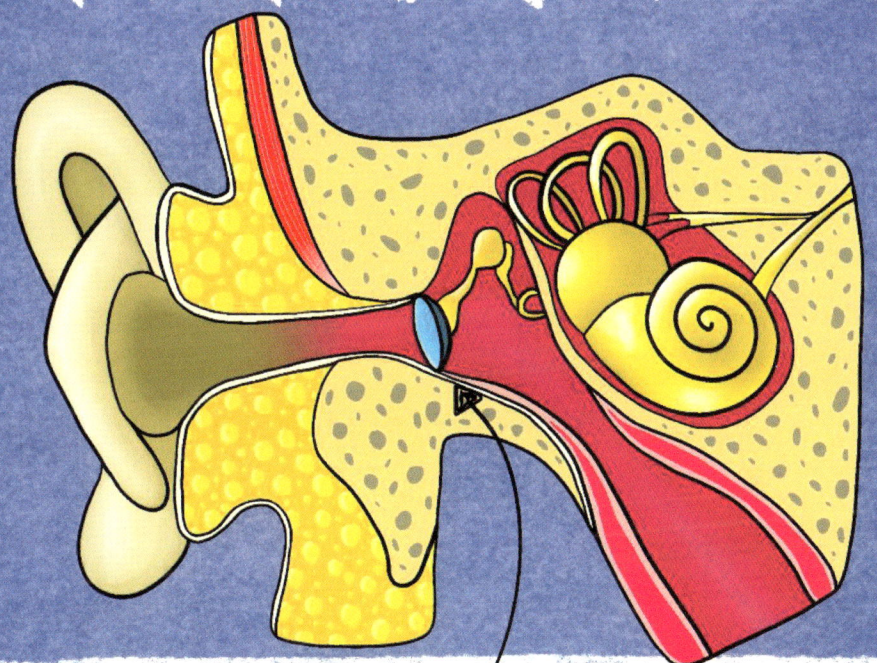

which helps you hear ringing bells

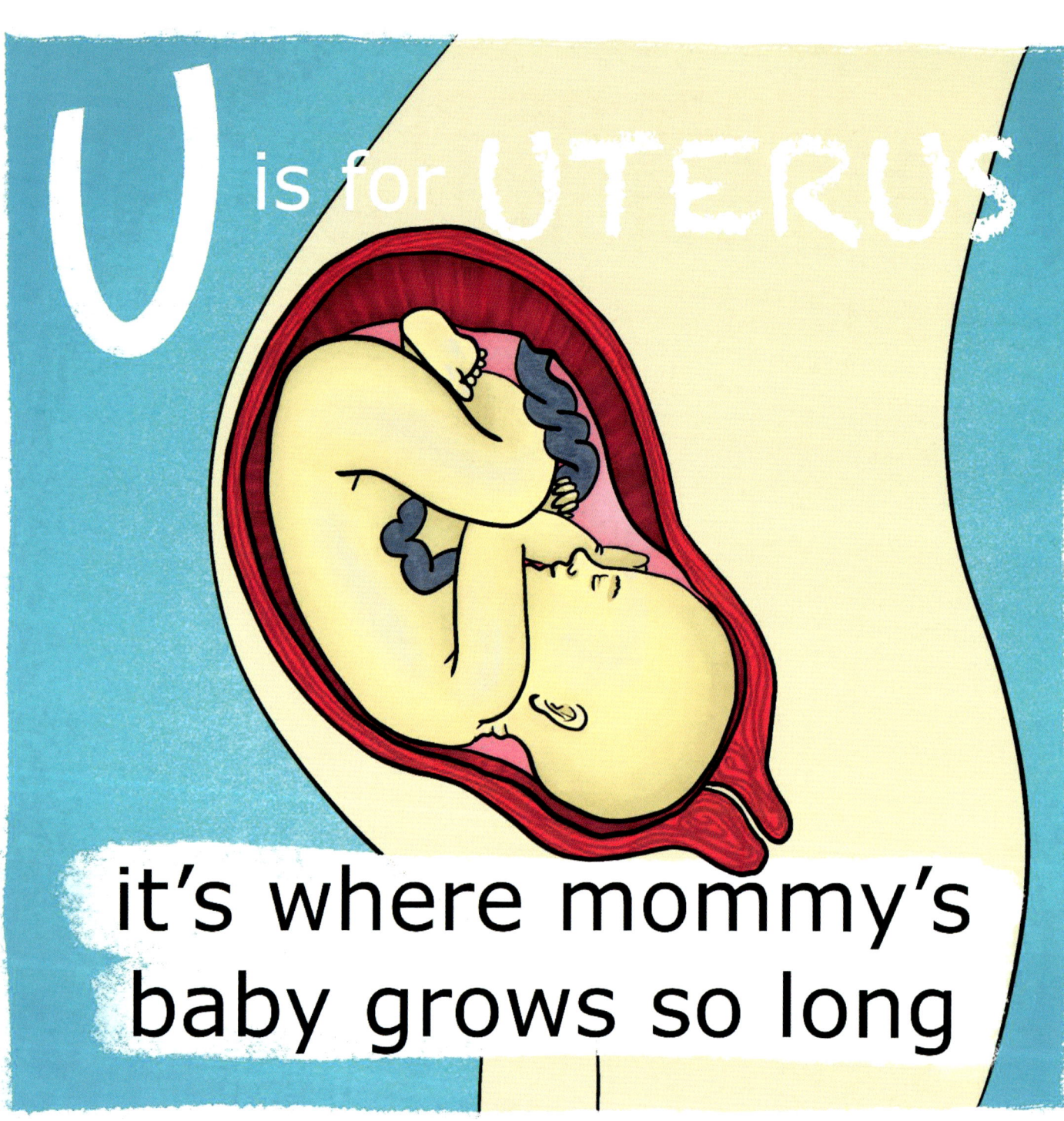

U is for UTERUS

it's where mommy's baby grows so long

V is for VENTRICLE

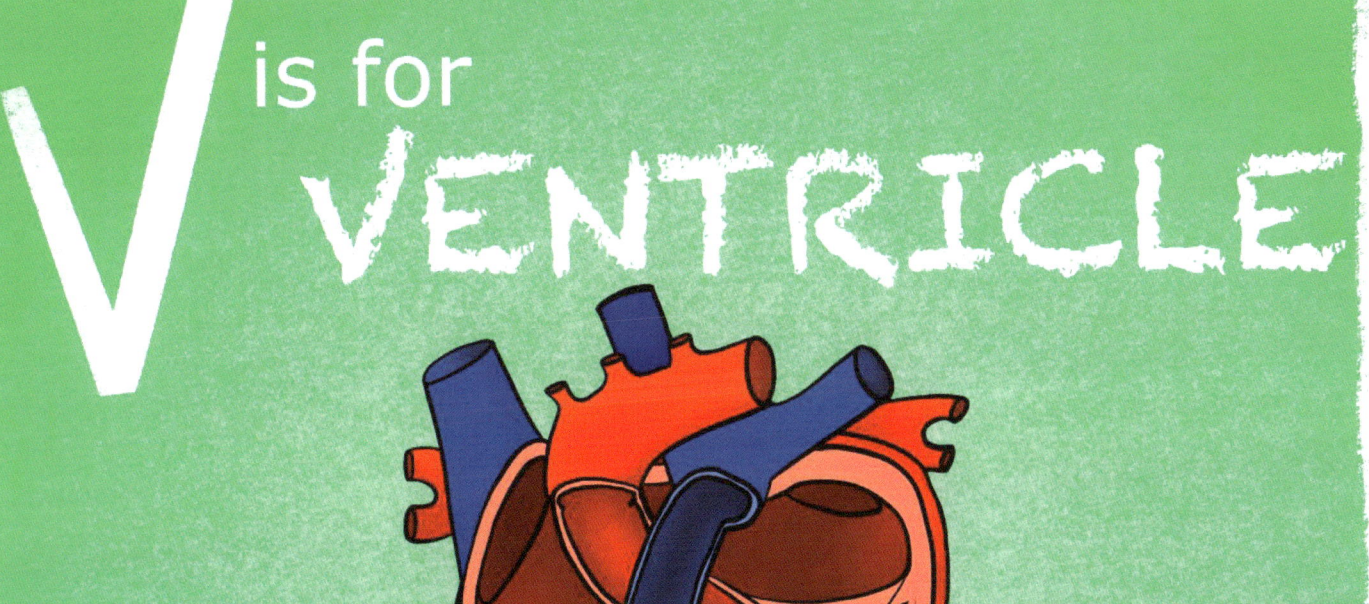

which pumps blood and
must be strong

X is for XIPHOID

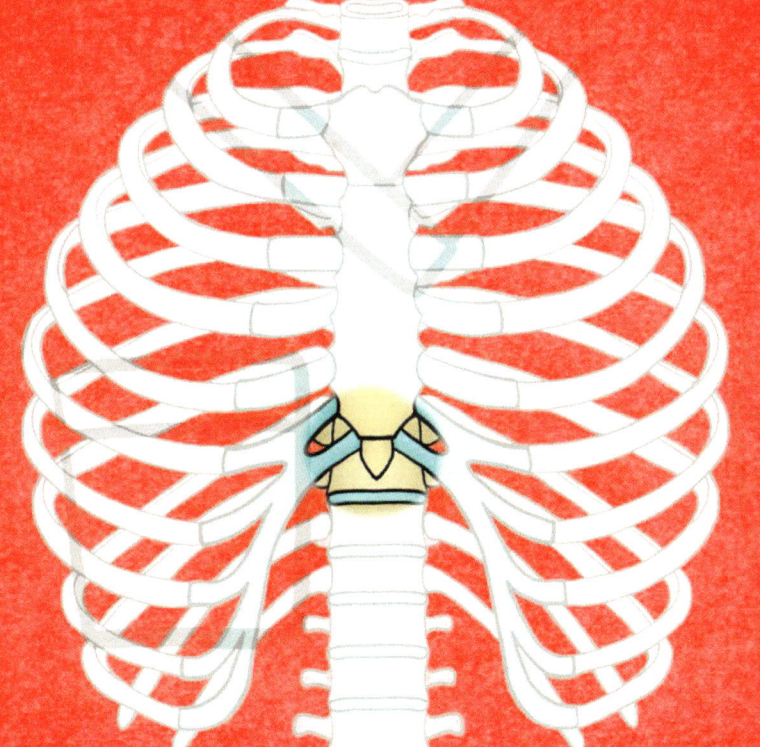

which sits just above your belly

Y is for YOLK SAC

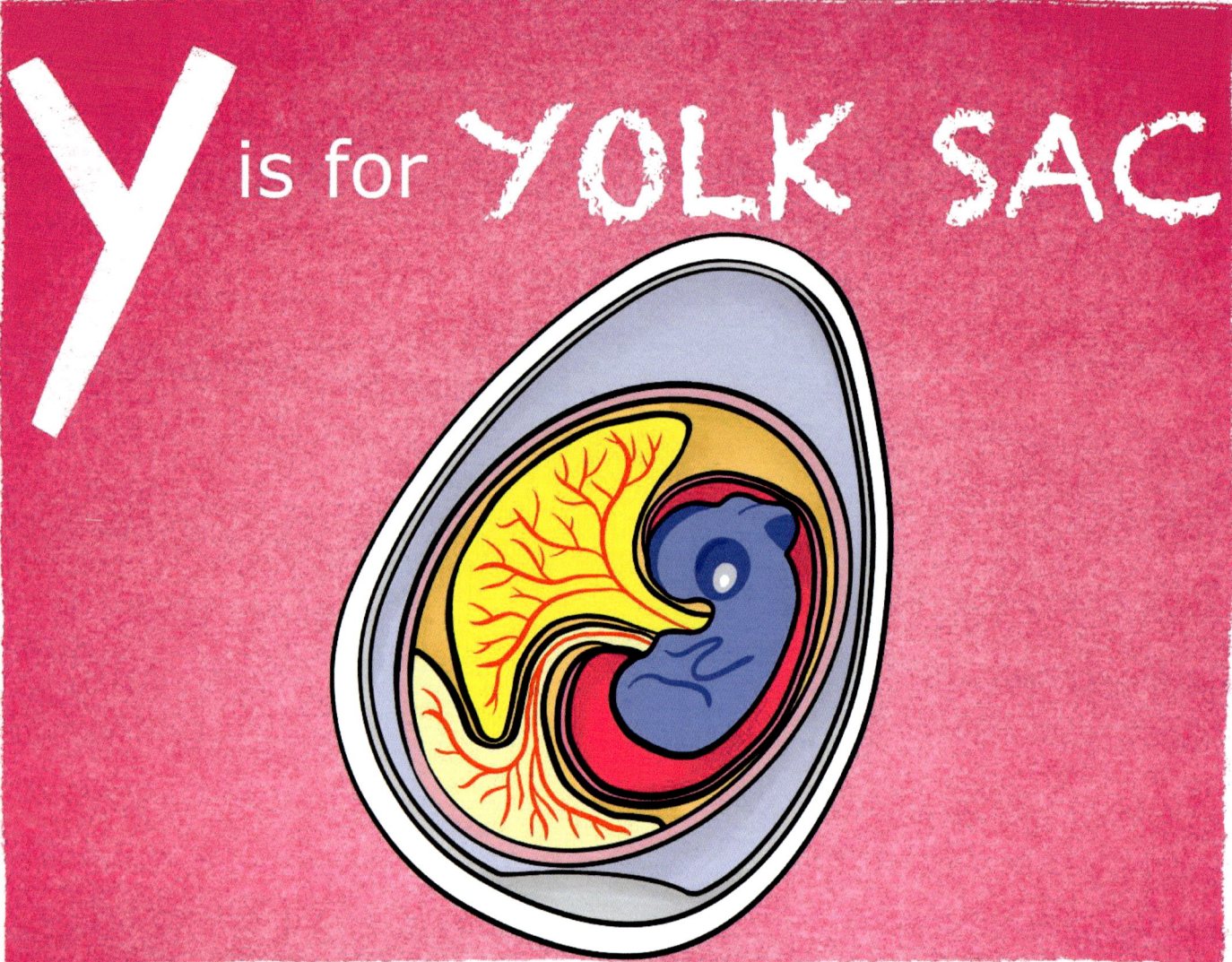

it gives a baby blood
for the first few weeks

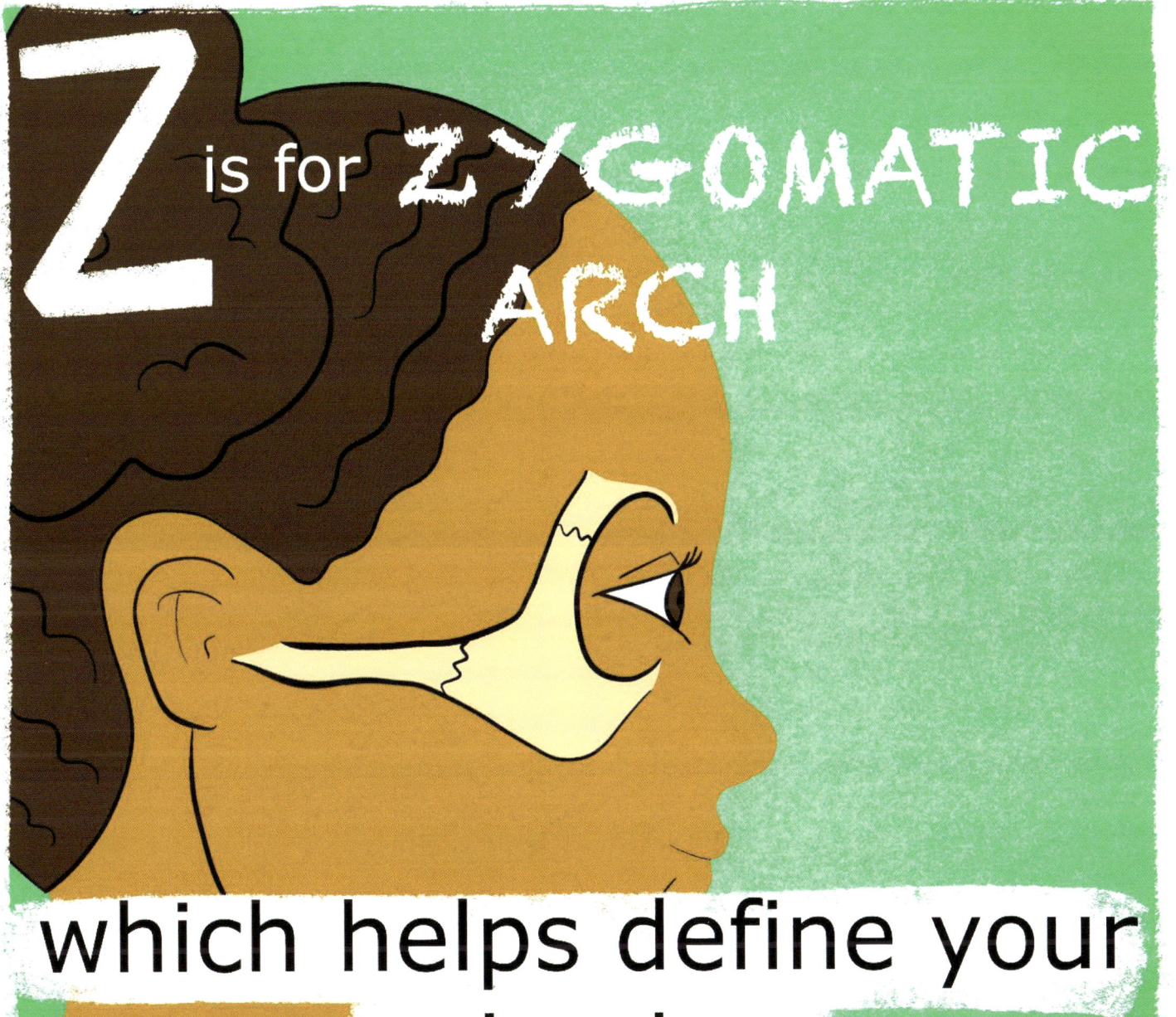

Z is for ZYGOMATIC ARCH

which helps define your cheeks

now that you

know your

anatomy

ABCs

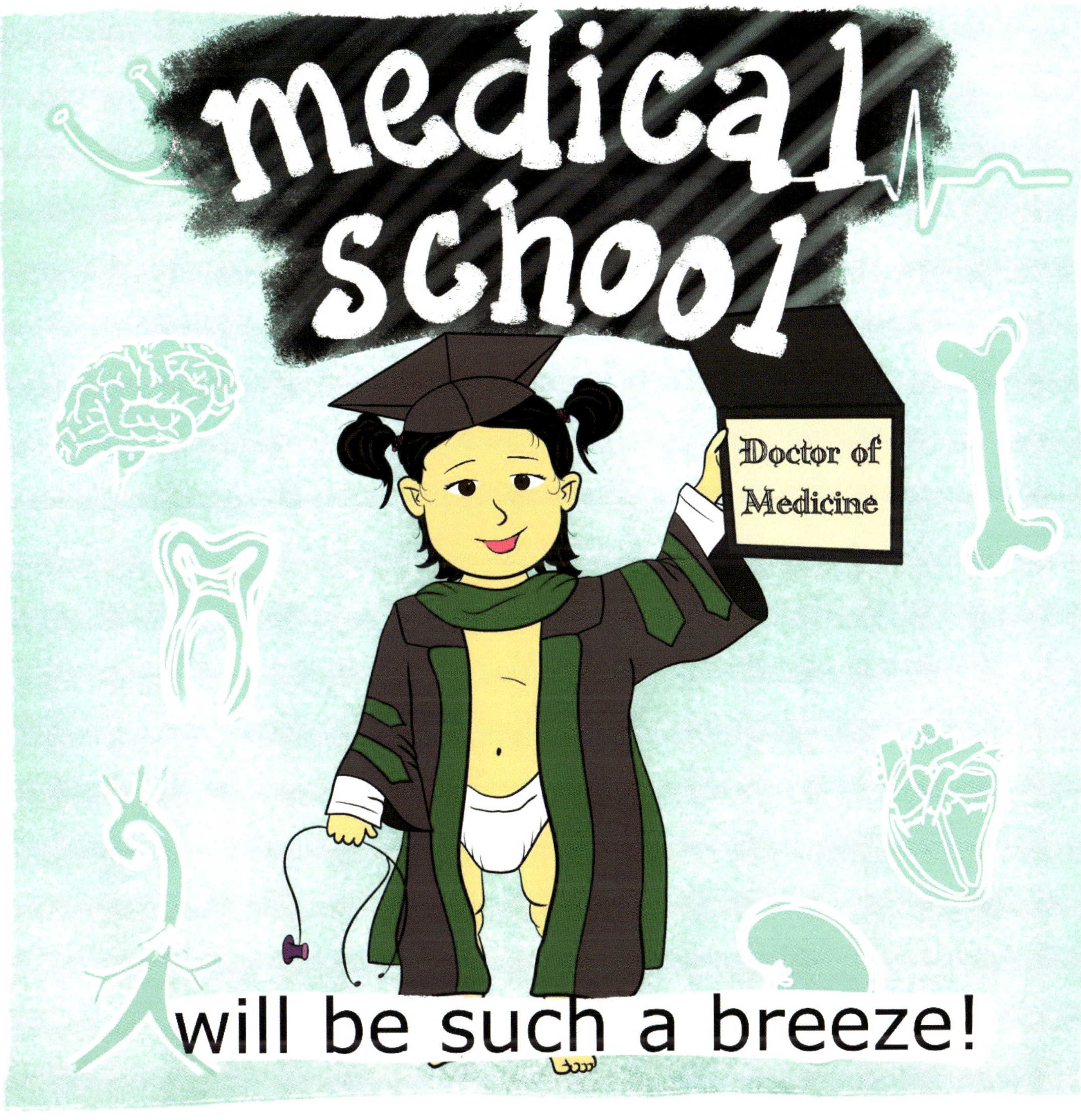
medical
school
Doctor of
Medicine
will be such a breeze!

Aorta Bone Marrow
Cerebellum Duodenum
Enamel Frontal Lobe
Gallbladder Hyoid Iris
Joints Kidney Lungs
Masseter Nares
Optic Nerve Patella
Quadriceps Ribs Spleen
Tympanic Membrane
Uterus Ventricle Wrist
Xiphoid Yolk Sac
Zygomatic Arch